FALL TO THE TOP

A TALE OF DEATH, DECEIT AND ONE MAN'S DESIRE TO HAVE IT ALL!

Peter Hirst

"For my muse" - P

ABOUT THE AUTHOR

Peter Hirst is a multi-skilled writer, director, producer, and actor who loves storytelling that explores the darkly comedic and intellectually challenging. From a childhood in the West Midlands, Birmingham, Peter's artistic path started with a course in the arts at college, where he developed a passion for creativity. But his journey took a different turn as he spent years accumulating valuable life experience working in manual jobs, adopting the strength and worldview of the working class.

Despite this time away, Peter never forsook his artistic foundation. When he returned to his artistic vocation, he did so with relentless energy, immediately diving into writing books, scripts, and literature with his dark humour. His writing demonstrates a profound knowledge of human nature, honed by both his artistic education and his time in the real world. Whether writing engaging stories or bringing them to life on screen, Peter's commitment to storytelling is central to everything, he does, making him a unique voice in modern fiction and film.

INTRODUCTION

"Fall to the Top" is more than a story; it is a raw, unfiltered look into a world where survival is not an option but a necessity. Growing up in different parts of the UK, I witnessed first-hand the struggles of those who dared to dream beyond their circumstances. This book is for them, for those who crave more from life and refuse to be defined by where they come from.

This novel had to feel as brutal as the streets. It's based on gritty, violent, and undeniably real experiences. I grew up in places where hardship was normal, ambition was met with resistance, and resilience was born. Those memories, those encounters, they fuel every page of this book.

Now, I feel the drive to bring these stories to life, not life – not just as fiction but as a testament to the strength, it takes to rise against the odds.

Welcome to Fall To The Top. This is more than a book. It's a fight for something greater.

Table of Contents

PROLOGUE

The city never slept. Its alleys breathed with whispered deals and quiet violence, and its streets pulsed with the desperation of men who had nothing and wanted everything. It was a world where the underworld was a machine built on greed, betrayal, and blood, a kingdom where power wasn't given; it was taken.

Mickey O'Brien understood that.

He wasn't at the top. Not yet. He was just another name in the dirt, another runner-pushing product for men who would never say his name twice. However, he had ambition, a hunger that burned deeper than the cold night air that wrapped around the estate's concrete bones.

Mickey stood against the brick wall of a narrow alley, hood up, one foot resting against the wall, under the dim glow of a flickering streetlamp. The city was alive with its usual sounds: the idling engines of cars in the distance, the chatter of club-goers, and the occasional screech of tyres as someone quickly escaped.

This part of town was built for men of a cultivated Ilk, who were never questioned but obeyed. Mickey had watched enough of how things were done: who was paid, who was left behind and who disappeared when they stepped out of line. He wasn't dumb. He knew how this game played. The bottom stayed at the bottom, and the top ensured that.

Tonight was like every other. A kid — barely older than sixteen — approached, shifting nervously, hands buried deep in his pockets.

"You got two grams?" The voice was barely above a whisper, eyes darting down the alley.

Mickey smirked. "Do I look like I'm standing here for the fresh air?"

The kid hesitated, looking over his shoulder before handing over a crumpled wad of notes. Mickey took his time, counting each bill, letting the kid squirm before slipping a small bag into his hand.

"Go on then," Mickey, muttered. "And don't be stupid."

The kid scurried off, swallowed by the night.

Mickey took a deep breath and rolled his shoulders. This life—it wasn't forever. He was sick of being at the bottom and taking orders from men who thought they were above the law. He had seen their mistakes, their arrogance. He knew their weaknesses.

Loyalty meant nothing here. Power was all that mattered.

A black car rolled by the alley entrance, slowing enough so Mickey could see silhouettes inside. Luther. The man who ran this part of the city. He is aHe is a king in his own right, with an air of fear and respect in equal measure from everyone he encounters.

Mickey's fingers curled into fists. He wouldn't be another nameless soldier in someone else's empire.

He had his own plans.

Soon, the streets would know his name.

CHAPTER 1:
A NIGHT IN THE STREETS

Cold air hung on Mickey O'Brien's body as he stood against a moist brick alley wall, resting his foot on the edge of it, his hands shoved deep inside the pockets of his black hoodie. The light from the distant streetlamp upon the corner stretched out its gold over the sidewalk, piercing into the quiet despair that seemed so evident in all the corners of the city. It was another business night, another waiting night, another disappointment night.

Mickey wasn't anywhere he wanted to be. Not yet.

Footsteps of the next buyer crunched through the alley. The kid was jittery—hands tucked deep into pockets, shoulders hunched against the night. He wasn't foreign to it, but there was still this look, and Mickey couldn't help but smirk over it. Desperate soul trying to find an exit, another piece in a game Mickey was determined to win.

"You got two grams?" the lad mumbled, his voice barely a whisper. His eyes darted nervously around the alley. He shifted from foot to foot, his restless energy betraying his anxiety.

Mickey cocked his head, his normal cocky attitude falling easily into place. "You think I'm out here for the view?" His tone was smooth, even a low growl that held an undertone of command. He wasn't a man to be messed with, even if his current situation made it seem otherwise. "One-fifty."

The child complained, grudgingly accepting the cost, and pulled out the money, a crumpled mass of bills that he jammed into Mickey's hand. The exchange was quick and unhurried, a routine transaction in the shadowy recesses of the city. It was completed, just another faceless transaction in the city's hidden world.

"Don't have to be a prick about it," the boy muttered, resentment coating his voice as he pushed the little bag into his pocket.

Mickey gave a low, mirthless laugh. "I'm going to own these streets one day," he repeated, his voice hard, unshakeable. It wasn't a threat but a statement of fact, a declaration of intent. "Watch your mouth and show some respect."

The boy vanished into the darkness, his footsteps echoing into the distance, leaving Mickey alone again. He breathed out, creating a cloud of white in the cold air. The anger that burned within him was a familiar friend, a reminder of his present abilities.

This wasn't where he was supposed to be. This wasn't the life he'd imagined for himself. However, it was a stepping stone, a temporary diversion from his way to something more. He'd wasted too many years watching others get ahead, watching others set the rules for him. He was done being a spectator, done being put on the sidelines.

A shiny black vehicle, tinted windows covering the passengers, drove by the alleyway. Individuals who had already reached the top of the hierarchy and ran the city's profitable underworld owned the car, a status symbol and representation of wealth. Mickey watched it round the corner, his gaze following it like a hawk pursuing its victim. He recognized the players, the power brokers, the men who made the real money. He recognized the game's rules, the complex web of alliances and betrayals that ruled the city's underworld. And he was tired of being on the bottom, just another face in the crowd.

The anger was not frustration, not in that raw, out-of-control manner. It was a slow-smouldering one, a building resentment driven by ambition. He was not satisfied with leftovers, with the crumbs that dropped from the tables of the mighty. He wanted better. He wanted everything.

He rebelliously drew his hood deeper onto his head and left the alleyway into the city's centre. The streets lay open before him, a maze of steel and stone, a battleground where fortunes rose and fell. He had waited long enough. He had suffered long enough. It was time to rise.

The city was his arena with all its dark secrets and hidden places. He would walk its mean streets, study its complex rules, and exploit its vulnerabilities. He would fight, claw, and climb to the top until he was among the best and had the respect he had earned. He would own these streets, not as a minor dealer, but as a king, a monarch of his own kingdom. And he would begin tonight. The cold air, once a foe, now felt like a challenge, a reminder of the barriers he would break. He was Mickey O'Brien, and he was taking it all.

CHAPTER 2:
THE CLUB ENCOUNTER

Bass from the speaker thumped hard through the air, shaking floorboards and even rattled glassware on top of the bar counter. Strobe lights were a blur in wildly erratic pulses through the black. The whole air reeked of booze, cheap perfume, or something darker–the smell that unmistakably defines business being consummated within the dark confines.

Mickey leaned against the bar, sipping whiskey neat, and his sharp gaze cut through the crowd. The club was packed, bodies swaying in reckless abandon, lost in the music. However, Mickey wasn't here for a good time. He was here for something bigger.

His eyes scanned the room until they landed on her.

Kiera.

She was nothing like the typical girls that flowed through these clubs, those who were drawn by the scent of danger as moths are drawn to a flame. There was a sharpness about her, something careful in how she moved. She was confident, but not that type of confidence that needed to be announced. She was magnetic, even if she didn't intend to be.

Mickey smirked and pushed off the bar, weaving through the crowd until he was close enough to speak.

"How're ya?" he said smoothly, leaning in just enough to be heard over the music.

Kiera turned, eyes flicking over him, assessing. A slow smile spread across her lips. "Hey, I'm good, you?"

"Better now."

She laughed, shaking her head. "That your line?"

Mickey grinned. "No, my usual line's worse."

"Oh? Let's hear it then."

Well, is there any Irish in ya?"

She arched an eyebrow, amused. "No, why?"

Mickey leaned in closer, lowering his voice. "Did you want some?"

Kiera burst out laughing, shaking her head in disbelief. "You're very upfront, aren't you?"

"I'm a direct kinda guy.

The moment felt easy, even in a place like this. The two of them made their way onto the dance floor, and Mickey forgot everything else for a while. They danced, they kissed, and for a few minutes, the weight of the streets, the hustle, and the hunger seemed to matter none.

Then the doors opened.

And the air in the club shifted.

Luther had arrived.

The moment he stepped in, the room bent to accommodate his energy. He was tall and broad, with a fitted black suit that gave him a semblance of intimidating. The air seemed to breathe, with his presence radiating a confidence borne out of knowledge: no one would dare stand in his way.

Luke, his right-hand enforcer, walked beside him like a shadow, cold and calculating, his eyes scanning the room for threats. Kenny, a step behind them, followed like a loyal dog, always present, always useful, but never truly one of them.

The crowd parted as Luther and his entourage strode toward the VIP section, where champagne was already being poured and where girls were already waiting.

Mickey glanced at them, his jaw tightening.

That was where he wanted to be.

That was where he should be.

Kiera must have caught his expression because she leaned in and whispered, "You know them?"

Mickey didn't take his eyes off Luther. "Not yet."

She studied him for a moment. "Be careful what you wish for."

The girls started to leave shortly thereafter. Kiera exchanged her number with Mickey before she gave him a mischievous grin. "Sure you don't wanna stay mine tonight?" he asked half-jokingly.

"Easy, tiger," she grinned. "Let's grab a coffee sometime."

Mickey grinned. "I'll hold you to that."

Kiera walked off into the darkness.

Mickey wasn't quitting that early.

He returned to the bar where his mates were ordering their next round.

"Boys, see the stunner I pulled?" he boasted.

"Yeah, fair play to ya," one of them chuckled.

"You not chasing her?" another asked.

Mickey smirked, rolling his shoulders. "She'll come running, man."

"Cocky prick."

"I'm Irish, she can't resist."

They all laughed, clinking shot glasses before downing their drinks.

Then someone nudged him.

"Fancy something stronger?"

Mickey turned, eyeing the guy. "What you mean?"

"Cheeky sniff?"

Mickey hesitated. "You got some?

"Nah, but that big fella over there with the entourage? He's known for it."

Mickey followed the guy's gesture, his eyes locking onto Luther's booth.

He didn't need to be told twice.

Outside the smoking area, the rain drizzled lightly over the small, dimly lit space. Mickey stepped out, letting the cold air hit his face. He reached into his pocket for a cigarette, but a voice spoke from the shadows before he could light it.

"You looking for something?"

Mickey turned.

Kenny stood there, watching him.

"Hey man, how're ya?" Mickey said casually.

Kenny inhaled from his cigarette, blowing smoke into the wet air. "Good, cheers, man."

"Do you work here?"

Kenny smiled. "In a way."

"You don't sound too sure." Mickey laughs

Kenny looked him over for a moment before cutting to the chase. "Is there something you want?"

Mickey grinned. "Whoa, I'm just pulling ya pisser, chill out, big man."

Kenny flicked the ash off his cigarette. "I offer certain services round here.

Mickey raised an eyebrow. "I'm flattered, but I don't swing that way, man."

Kenny chuckled, shaking his head. "You're a cocky one, huh?"

"I'm stood out here for a reason."

Kenny nodded slowly. "I sell drugs. Uppers, downers, whatever you need."

Mickey tilted his head. "That makes more sense."

"It sell well?"

Kenny's expression darkened slightly. "I'm the main street distributor round here. Luther's the big boss. We own this area.

Mickey digested the words.

Luther didn't run some club. He was the man. That is the tip of the iceberg.

"Very mafia," Mickey said coolly. "How much is a gram of coke?"

"£80."

Kenny reached into his pocket and pulled out a small pouch of white powder. He passed it to Mickey, his fingers touching Mickey's for half a second.

A test.

Mickey didn't pause to think. He took the pouch and shoved it into his pocket.

Kenny then pressed a small slip of paper into his palm. "If you ever want some work, hit me up."

Mickey looked at the number scribbled across it, feeling the weight of the opportunity in his hands.

Ambition flared in his chest.

This was it.

The first step toward something bigger.

He glanced back at the club, toward Luther's VIP booth, and then flicked his cigarette into the rain.

This city would know his name.

And this was just the beginning.

CHAPTER 3:
A TASTE OF THE LIFE

The morning light filtered through the half-closed blinds, casting soft lines across Mickey's unmade bed. He lay there, wide awake, his heart beating against his ribs in a restless rhythm. It wasn't a hangover that clouded his senses; he hadn't had much to drink. Still, a thick haze lingered in his mind, fuelled by the memory of Kenny's smooth, self-assured smile under the club's flickering lights.

Kenny had moved through the crowd effortlessly as if the chaotic pulse of the club bent to his will. Mickey had been captivated by his presence, the kind that made you forget everything else in the room. When Kenny leaned in, casually slipping a small bag of white powder into Mickey's hand as if it was just spare change, his voice was low, almost daring.

"Hit me up if you're interested," Kenny said, sliding a crumpled business card between Mickey's fingers with a wink before disappearing into the sea of bodies.

In the cold clarity of morning, that single act felt like an invitation, a doorway to something darker, edgier, and maybe even dangerous. Yet, instead of rejecting the thought outright, Mickey found himself drawn to it, questioning whether curiosity, defiance, or loneliness was driving that persistent tug in his chest.

The bag still sat in his jacket pocket, untouched but impossibly heavy. Mickey's fingers itched with indecision. He knew he should throw it away, pretend the encounter had never happened. However, deep down, he wasn't sure if he wanted to.

The clang of tools and the grinding sound of heavy machinery echoed across the construction site as Mickey hauled a wheelbarrow full of cement mix across the uneven ground. Sweat dripped from his brow, and his muscles screamed under the weight. His back ached, but what gnawed at him more was the growing resentment brewing inside.

He paused near the edge of the site, resting against the handles of the wheelbarrow as he watched the supervisor shout orders from afar. The man stood tall and smug in his pristine high-visibility jacket, clipboard in hand, barking commands like royalty.

Mickey gritted his teeth. This isn't it. This can't be it, he thought with bitter words. Every day on this site felt like a slow death—the same repetitive tasks and condescending voices treating him like dirt under their boots. He was better than this. He had to be better than this. Yet, here he was, breaking his back for crumbs while men like Kenny walked around with pockets full of cash, respected and feared.

"Oi, Mickey!" a voice barked. The supervisor. "Get your arse in gear or you're out on your ear!"

Mickey's jaw tightened. The urge to snap back, to throw the wheelbarrow down and tell the supervisor to shove it, nearly overwhelmed him. However, he knew better. He needed this job—for now.

As he walked back across the site, his mind turned to Kenny's words: "I'm the main street distributor round here. Luther's the big boss. We own this area."

There was power in those words, raw and undeniable. Kenny didn't wear steel-toed boots or haul cement. He didn't bow his head to anyone—except maybe Luther. And that, Mickey realized, was what he craved more than anything: power, respect, freedom.

By lunchtime, Mickey had made up his mind.

The door to Kenny's modest suburban house creaked open, revealing the drug dealer in a wrinkled Hawaiian shirt and joggers. Mickey raised an eyebrow.

"Not what I expected," Mickey remarked dryly.

Kenny grinned. "What, thought I'd be in a dingy warehouse with flickering lights?" He gestured to Mickey inside. "Get in before the neighbours start talking."

The interior was surprisingly ordinary—children's toys scattered across the floor, family photos lining the walls, and the scent of freshly brewed coffee lingering in the air.

"Want a brew?" Kenny offered as they entered the kitchen, where bundles of cocaine sat openly on the table alongside scales and packaging materials.

"Black, no sugar," Mickey replied, trying to mask his nerves.

Kenny chuckled. "Good choice. Coffee's strong enough to put hair on your chest."

As Kenny poured the coffee, a young man entered the room. "This is Paul," Kenny introduced. "Been with me for years. Knows the streets like the back of his hand. Makes a banging vegan cheesecake, too."

Mickey nodded politely. "Alright, mate?"

Paul grinned. "Welcome to the business."

Kenny set the coffee down in front of Mickey and leaned against the counter, his tone shifting to something more serious. "So, you want in?"

Mickey didn't hesitate. "Yeah. I'm done breaking my back for peanuts. I want more."

Kenny nodded approvingly. "Good. However, know this, working for me means working for Luther. He's not the kind of guy you cross. You fly right, you will do just fine. Step outta line, you'll wish you hadn't."

Mickey sipped his coffee, the bitter taste grounding him. "What's the cut?"

"Two percent," Kenny said flatly.

Mickey furrowed his brow. "Two percent? We're taking all the risk."

Kenny's face grew sombre. "You don't import it. You don't cultivate it. You don't pay off cops or filter the goods. You stand on a corner and sell. That's the easy part, and for that, you get two percent. Take it or leave it."

The weight of Kenny's words lingers in the air. Mickey knew to him that there was no room for negotiation.

"I'm in," he said firmly.

Kenny's lips curled into a sly smile. "Good. Paul will show you the ropes. You do your job right, and who knows? Maybe one day you'll climb the ladder. "As Mickey left Kenny's house later that day, a glint of ambition burned in his eyes. He knew this was only the first step toward something bigger.

No more labouring under the sun. No more barking supervisors.

This city would know his name.

Chapter 4:
Deeper Connections

Mickey's induction into Kenny's operation was seamless. He learned quickly, the trade, the risks, and most of all, the power that came with it. The high of earning money without harming his back on a construction site was addictive. Each sale he made, each new customer he acquired, solidified his status in the underworld.

The streets spoke his name now, but only hesitantly. He wasn't Kenny yet, far from it, certainly not Luther, but he was on the upswing. The work never ended, long nights, high-risk transactions, and the occasional flash of violence, but Mickey didn't mind. He lived for it. He had once been a faceless drudge, and now he was a man who commanded notice, respect, and growing fear.

However, not everyone was impressed.

Kiera stood at the entrance to their apartment, her arms crossed tightly over her chest as if she was preparing herself for a chill she couldn't shake. The knot in her stomach had settled there a long time before she had stepped inside, but seeing Mickey like this—slumped over a stack of money, barely looking up at her, made it settle deeper, like a rock.

Her eyes, once soft and full of trust, now bore the weight of too many late nights waiting up, unanswered phone calls, and excuses that barely held together. She used to look at him and see the boy she fell in love with, the one who would pull her close in the kitchen just to dance, who made her laugh even when she didn't want to, who used to talk about their future like it was something they were building together.

Now, when she looked at him, she saw all the shadows.

The shadows under his eyes, the shadows of where he wouldn't take her, the shadows of people whose names made her skin crawl. In addition, worst of all, the shadow of the man he used to be.

Something sharp twisted inside her, part concern, part outright anger. How did we get here? She wondered, though she already knew the answer. She had felt the shift happen in real-time, like sand slipping between her fingers, but she had told herself it wasn't permanent. That he would come back to her. Whatever this was, it was just a phase.

However, standing here now, watching him count money with that shut, expressionless face, she knew something that made her stomach knot.

Mickey wasn't lost. He wasn't drowning, waiting to be saved.

He had already made his choice.

And Kiera wasn't sure she could just stand there and watch him become a person she didn't recognize.

"You missed dinner. Again."

Mickey barely looked up from the clump of cash he was counting. His fingers moved with practised speed, stacking the bills into neat piles with an almost meditative intent.

"Got caught up," he muttered, not even bothering to explain.

Kiera scoffed, moving deeper into the room. "Yeah? Caught up doing what, exactly?"

He sighed, more annoyed than guilty, and slumped his shoulders, tossing the pile of cash onto the table with a soft thud. "Work, Kiera. You know how it is."

Kiera's eyes narrowed. "Something you want to share with me? Something that doesn't involve getting caught up in whatever it is you're doing out there?"

She laughed coldly, shaking her head. "Funny," she said coldly. "I remember when 'work' meant actual work. Now it's just you vanishing for hours, coming back smelling of smoke and booze, and acting like it doesn't matter."

That shut him up. He finally looked up to meet her eyes, his patience fraying. "I'm doing this for us," he said, voice unbreakable, as if sheer willpower would make her see it like he did. "So we don't have to get by anymore."

Kiera's face didn't change. "Get by?" she snapped. "We did just fine before. You had a job. A good job."

Mickey's teeth were locked together. "A good job that paid me peanuts," he growled. His fists curled as he leaned forward. "This? This is real money. Real power. No more getting pushed around. No more taking orders from pricks in hard hats who think they own me."

She breathed sharply, but there was no shock on her face. Only a tired kind of disappointment. "And what about taking orders from Kenny? From Luther?"

His jaw clicked shut. She had him there, and she knew it. However, he was not going to give in.

"It's different," he said, though the words sounded pathetic.

"Is it?" She stepped closer, her voice dropping to a lower, sharper pitch. "Or have you just traded one boss for another?"

The air was charged with tension. Mickey was the first to look away, his eyes furtive.

Kiera breathed slowly, deeply, as if trying to steel herself. When she spoke again, her voice was lower but no less unyielding.

"You wouldn't get it," Mickey muttered, running a hand over his face.

"No," she breathed. "I think I get it."

The air between them was thick with all the things they hadn't said and didn't know how to say anymore.

At last, Kiera spoke, drawing a deep breath. She turned, grabbed her coat from the back of the chair, and put it on with deliberate motions.

"I'm going to my sister's for a few days," she said, her voice shaking slightly but firm. "Perhaps by the time I get back, you'll remember who you used to be."

Mickey didn't attempt to detain her. He didn't call out to her or catch her hand. He didn't even turn around when the door slammed shut behind her.

Instead, he sat back, ran his hand through his hair, and stared at the money on the table.

She didn't get it.

However, one day, she would.

CHAPTER 5: POWER

The neon sign above Luther's Club flashed, its glow reflecting off the restless crowd of people standing outside. Music thumped through the doors within, the heavy bass resonating off the stone walls. A line of waiting patrons stood a block down the sidewalk, hungry for an evening of escape.

Mickey would not be waiting, however. He turned towards the side door and was out of sight without glancing at the line.

The backroom smelled of cigars and alcohol, a shadowy den of hushed words and illicit business. A group of men gathered around a table littered with cash, drugs, and empty glasses, their faces lost in the shadows. Luke, Luther's second-in-command, sat at the head of the table. He toyed with a knife, spinning it around his fingers with a sense of ease that conveyed experience—and danger.

Mickey glanced around the room cautiously. Kenny, already seated, nodded to him and beckoned him over. He could feel the men's eyes weighing on him as he approached, judging him before he could even speak.

"This is him," Kenny said, nodding in Mickey's direction. "The new guy."

Luke's gaze raked over him, unimpressed. Another fresh recruit. Another liability. His smirk was slow, deliberate, carrying the disdain that made it clear he had already judged Mickey and found him lacking.

"This the one you've been vouching for?" Luke's voice was rough, edged with scepticism. "Looks soft to me."

Mickey didn't flinch. He met Luke's stare and let a smirk of his own curve the corner of his mouth. "And you seem to be a man compensating for something."

A murmur ran through the room. Someone let out a laugh, and then they coughed it off. The others leaned forward, waiting for Luke's reaction. The way his fingers were stiffened on the knife let Mickey know he had hit a sensitive area.

"You've got a mouth," Luke murmured, rising slowly to his feet. His movements were measured and intentional—the kind that gave a man time to feel his impending mistake. "Let's see if you've got the guts to back it up."

Kenny shifted in his chair, giving Mickey a warning glance. "Easy, Luke. He's just getting started."

Luke ignored him, stepping closer to Mickey. "No, let him speak for himself."

Mickey kept his posture relaxed, but his voice was firm. "I'm here to work. Not to get into a pissing contest."

Luke's smirk widened. "Smart answer. But I'm not convinced." He gestured toward the chair opposite him. "Sit. Let's see if you've got more than just talk."

Mickey hesitated but took the seat. The tension in the room lingered, heavy and unspoken.

Luke inched forward, the knife flat on the table before him as he gazed at Mickey. "Ever had a real fight, kid?"

Mickey did not flinch. "More than one."

Luke's eyebrow rose, his face unyielding. "That so? Fights in the street don't count. I mean an honest fight. One where you're outnumbered. One where you don't just get to walk away in the end."

Mickey left the question hanging before answering. "I've fought to live. Is that good enough for you?"

Luke laughed, shaking his head. "We'll see." He picked up the knife again, spinning it idly. "Tell me something, Mickey. Why do you think you belong here?"

Mickey met his gaze. "Because I don't break easy."

The room fell silent once more, tension wrapping around them. Luke liked to poke, to probe for weakness and lay it bare for the whole world to see. But Mickey would not let him.

Before the situation could escalate further, the door swung open, and the room fell silent. Luther stepped inside, his presence commanding without effort. He didn't have to raise his voice for the entire mood to shift. It just did.

"You're here to work," Luther said, his gaze moving between them. "Not to make enemies."

Mickey didn't hesitate. "Crystal."

Luther nodded, mollified for the moment. "Kenny will fill you in." His eyes shifted to Luke, narrowed in unspoken threat. "And you—let it go."

Luke's smirk returned, but this time with something else behind it. He recognized the command, but the defiance in his eyes didn't falter. He stepped back, but not before patting Mickey on the back—a little too hard to be friendly. A message wrapped in feigned friendship.

"Welcome to the company, kid."

Mickey smiled robotically, but he wasn't fooled. The battle might have been postponed, but it was far from won. If he was going to survive here, he would have to be smarter than that. Luke hadn't yet proven himself to Mickey, and there could be a next time without a crowd around to keep things polite.

Kenny hit Mickey on the back as they exited the backroom, bringing him to the club's main floor. Music thumped harder here, drowning out most of the chatter. Kenny spoke in hushed tones.

"You'll have to be careful around Luke. He remembers things."

Mickey sneered. "So do I."

Kenny laughed for a moment. "That kind of attitude will land you very far or get you killed. Don't get the two confused."

They entered the bar, where Kenny ordered a drink. Mickey looked around at the customers, watching the type of man who would frequent an establishment like this—men with too much money, others with too much desperation. It was a mixture of power and vulnerability, and Mickey would find his position among the powerful.

"Ever worked a joint like this before?" Kenny asked, handing Mickey a drink.

"No," Mickey admitted. "But I'm quick on the uptake."

Kenny took a swig from his glass, studying him closely. "Good. Because this is more than just a club. It's a company. And if you wish to survive, you must be useful."

Mickey nodded, already understanding the blatant message. He wasn't here to party or to fritter his time away. He was here to rise up, and nobody would stand in his way.

He spun around to confront the room, locking eyes with Luke from where he stood in the club. The enforcer threw up a mock salute, his smirk still in place. Mickey returned the same, aware that Luke was only seeking an excuse.

Whatever lay ahead, Mickey was ready.

Chapter 6:
A Dangerous Game

Mickey had always craved more. For power. For control. For a life outside the streets that had shaped him. The money began coming in, and it was simple to rationalize taking a little bit for himself. Just a little at first—enough to dip his toes in the water to see if anyone cared. No one did. Therefore, he took a little more. Then more, it was a risky game, the one he played carefully.

Kenny, though, wasn't blind. He saw the figures not quite balancing out, the product's weight shifting in all the wrong ways. He wasn't the brightest bulb in the box, but he'd been around long enough to know when someone was skimping. And that someone was Mickey.

"You think I don't notice?" Kenny's voice was strained with anger, as he stood face-to-face with Mickey outside the club one night. The neon lights gave his face a yellowish tinge, his face contorted between rage and incredulity.

Mickey leaned against the wall, unmoved. "Notice what?"

"Don't play stupid with me, mate. You're embezzling. I don't know how much yet, but I know you are."

Mickey shrugged, a smirk pulling at the corner of his mouth. "If I was, what would you do about it?"

Kenny took another step forward, voice dropping to a growl. "Luther finds out, and you're a dead man."

"Luther doesn't need to know," Mickey retorted. "Think about it, Kenny. He's growing. He's busy. He's got bigger fish to fry than a couple of grand missing here and there."

Kenny's jaw set. He loved Luther, but terror was an intense force. And if Mickey were correct, and they might claim a greater portion for themselves, perhaps the risk was warranted. Yet, he did not like going up against Luther. No one did.

"This is a bad mistake," Kenny warned. "You do not play around with Luther's cash."

Mickey clapped him on the shoulder, feigning camaraderie. "Relax. I've got it under control."

But Kenny wasn't the only one keeping an eye on him.

Luther's office was dark, filled with the heavy scent of cigar smoke. A figure shifted in the corner, a person waiting too long. Mason. Luther's former mentor. The man who had once dominated the south side before he stepped aside and allowed his protégé to take the reins.

"You're getting sloppy," Mason said, his voice gravelly with age and discontent. "You let the rats run wild, and soon they'll be chewing through your empire."

Luther exhaled slowly, placing his cigar in the crystal ashtray. "Mickey?"

Mason nodded. "Your boy's got ambition. Dangerous ambition."

Luther didn't respond initially. He already knew Mickey was trouble, but he had been handy—swift, smart, and hard enough to fit into the operation. However, if Mason noticed, something had to be done about him.

"You want me to put him down?" Sitting in the corner leaning against the bar, Luke cracked his knuckles, as ever ready for violence.

Not yet," Luther replied, his eyes clouding. "He's a valuable pawn on the board, at least for now. But if he strays too far from the mark."

Mason smiled. "Then you do what needs to be done."

Luther sat back, his fingers drumming against the desk. "Watch him closely. If he falls, he's out.

Mickey did not know any of this. As far as he was concerned, he was rising to the top. He had Kenny on his toes, sure, but that would subside. The money was rolling in more quickly than ever before, and as long as he played his cards correctly, he would have enough influence to make a move when the time was right.

However, in this world, power was a capricious thing. And Mickey had made one crucial error—he believed he could outmanoeuvre Luther.

The game had started. He simply didn't know he was already losing.

For the next few weeks, Mickey worked his scheme carefully, just enough to keep his cut growing without drawing too much suspicion. Every time he pocketed a little extra cash, his confidence swelled. Kenny, however, wasn't so easily fooled.

"You're getting reckless," Kenny muttered one night as they stood near the club's loading dock. Trucks moved in and out, carrying shipments worth more than their lives. "I don't like this."

Mickey smiled, taking a cigarette out of his pack. "You worry too much."

"I've been around long enough to recognize when a man is testing his luck," Kenny retorted, his eyes sweeping the alley. "And you're testing it."

Mickey blew a cloud of smoke, his eyes unwavering. "I'm not backing down, Kenny. If you don't want in, then get out of the way."

Kenny ran a hand through his hair in frustration. "You don't understand, do you? There is no 'stepping down.' If Luther finds out, I'm dead just for knowing about it."

Mickey snubbed his cigarette, moving closer to Kenny. It may be time we didn't take orders from him anymore.

Kenny's eyes grew wide. "You've lost your fucking mind."

Mickey chuckled. "Or perhaps I'm finally seeing things clearly."

Meanwhile, Mason watched Luther's operation, noting every change and deviation from the usual. One night, he met Luther again in the club's private lounge, where thick walls muffled the music and luxury surrounded them.

"You're waiting too long," Mason said, sipping whiskey. "You let a weed grow too long, and it spreads."

Luther stirred his drink contemplatively. "Mickey believes he's above the law. That makes him careless. Let him think he's winning."

Mason raised an eyebrow. "And then?"

Luther's smile was ice-cold. "Then we remind him of who he's playing with."

The initial warning was silence. A couple of regulars Mickey had been working with disappeared—no calls, no texts. The second warning was explicit. One of Kenny's sources was discovered in an alley, beaten beyond identification.

Kenny took Mickey by the arm outside the club that evening, his grip firm. "This is getting out of hand. You need to quit."

Mickey pulled his arm away. "I'm not quitting."

"Then you're signing your own death warrant," Kenny hissed. "Luther's coming for you."

Mickey's jaw clenched. He knew Kenny was right. However, he wasn't about to back down now. Not when he was so close.

The trap was set.

Mickey entered the club that evening, anticipating business as usual. Instead of the usual din of sound, he was met with an unsettling silence. There was no raucous music, no laughter, but only the insidious hum of tension. Kenny hovered by the bar, his expression inscrutable.

Then he caught sight of him.

In the VIP booth, Luther stared back at him with cold amusement. In addition, beside him, Mason.

Mickey's heart racing, he compelled himself forward. "Boss," he said with an air of nonchalance.

Luther did not respond immediately. Instead, he pointed to the chair on the other side of the room and said, "Sit."

Mickey delayed and then sat. He felt Luke behind him, a subtle but unyielding threat.

Luther rested his elbows on the table. "Tell me, Mickey... am I stupid?"

Mickey gulped hard. He had made his move. Now, he waited to determine if he had lost the entire game.

CHAPTER 7:
THE COST OF BETRAYAL

The air in the darkened room was tense; the only sound was the steady drumming of Luther's fingers on the highly polished tabletop. Mickey's heart beat wildly against his ribcage, a desperate drumbeat against the coming doom he felt closing in. Luther leaned forward, elbows heavy on the table, fingers linked, creating a cage around the unspoken menace in the air. "Tell me, Mickey... am I stupid?" he said, voice low and convincingly calm.

Mickey gulped, his throat dry and tight. He had made his ploy and staked everything on a calculated gamble. Now, he had to find out if he had lost the whole game if his ambition had led him to a fatal miscalculation. He tried to force a chuckle, a desperate attempt to mask the fear that gnawed at his insides, but it came out as a strained, hollow sound. "Come on, boss," he stammered, his voice betraying his anxiety. "You know you're the smartest in the room."

Luther's eyes held steady, undeterred by the insipid flattery. "Well, then explain to me why you thought I wouldn't mind," he goaded, piercing Mickey with an unyielding stare. His eyes sought the slightest crack in the armour of deception.

Mickey's belly knotted in fear. "Mind what?" he asked, stalling, trying to fabricate a coherent lie.

Luke's fingers wrapped around his shoulder, his hold hard and threatening. "Don't demean him," he warned, his voice a growl, his hold squeezing, and a hurting reminder of his strength.

Luther inched forward, his face inches from Mickey's, and his hot breath warming his skin. "You've been short-changing, cross-selling, and stealaling for yourself," he stated, his voice thick with cold, controlled rage. He inclined his head toward Mason, his taciturn partner, before focusing on Mickey. "And now you're here, staring me in the face like you still have options."

Mickey's mouth was dry, his tongue heavy and thick. "Boss, that's not—" he started, but his speech was interrupted by Mason's voice, low and firm.

"Lying to a man such as Luther is worse than theft from him," Mason went on, his eyes boring into Mickey's, scanning him with a frigid, calculating intensity. "So tell me. Are you a liar, too?"

Mickey's heart raced in his ears, the noise thunderous, deafening all else. He had to think fast and come up with an escape from this impossible predicament. He breathed slowly, deliberately, affecting an air of tired resignation. "Listen," he started, his tone flat and firm, "I made some plays, yeah. Not on you, though. On Kenny. He was the one stealing from you. I just... got my piece before he ran the whole thing into the ground."

Luther's expression did not change, but he and Mason shared a glance, a wordless message that left Mickey suspended in anguished suspense. He did not know if it was an omen of hope or a sentence of death.

Mason sat back in his chair; his eyes squinted, weighing Mickey as a man calculates the chances of a gamble. "Interesting," he said, his tone filled with distrust.

Luther drummed his fingers against the table, the rhythmic tapping a chilling counterpoint to Mickey's frantic beating heart. "Kenny, huh?" he asked, his voice deceptively casual.

Mickey nodded, seizing the sliver of opportunity. "Yeah. Ask around. You'll see I'm right," he said, his voice gaining confidence.

Luther exhaled slowly and measuredly, his eyes fixed on Mickey's. Then, without warning, he snapped his fingers at Luke.

Luke pulled Mickey out of his seat, a grip of iron on his arm, and jammed his head onto the table, the sudden movement causing a spasm of pain through his neck.

"Here's the thing," Luther stated, his voice flat, free of emotion. "If you're lying, you'll die screaming."

Mickey ground his teeth; his jaw clamped shut as Luke pressed down, ramming his face further into the hard surface of the table.

Luther gestured toward Mason. "What do you think?" he growled, his voice low.

Considering the horse race odds, Mason tilted his head, weighing Mickey like a man. Eternity passed between them, each moment a living hell for Mickey. Then, at last, Mason spoke. "Let's try out his story," he said, his tone dripping with an icy finality.

Luther smiled a hungry smile that made Mickey's skin crawl. "Good idea," he replied, his tone dripping with sadistic humour.

Mickey's face hardly flickered, but a shadow flashed across his eyes—fast, keen, like a knife blade flashing in the sun. He had always had a talent for concealing fear, covering it with layers of cold calculation and hollow smiles. But at this moment, he wasn't fooling anyone.

Luther's words had cut deep. The threat was not idle, and Mickey was aware of it. Aware that Luther was the type of man who would carry through on his promise to the end. But for all the flash of fear in his stomach and the creeping chill along his spine, Mickey compelled himself to stand firm. It's because fear was not enough, on its own, to make a man change.

He had clawed his way to the top with bloody hands, cut backroom deals that would never see the light of day, and reduced men to spectres without losing a wisp of sleep. The money, the influence, the empire he had constructed—it wasn't something he could simply abandon. Not because he didn't want to but because men like him did not get to.

Therefore, he swallowed his fear and let it drop into his belly like a swallowed stone.

"Luther," Mickey said, his voice suave, honed, a knife blunted just enough to conceal its point. "You don't frighten me."

It was a lie. A lie they both knew.

Luther just smiled because he knew something Mickey wouldn't accept—fear was not surrender. Mickey was scared, sure. But fear wouldn't compel him to give up. It would only make him more lethal.

CHAPTER 8:
MICKEY'S AMBITION TAKES OVER

The club was not only a meeting ground but also a universe in itself, a maddening chasm of ambition and decadence. Each dimly lit neon sign sent shadows stretching and twisting like snakes, speaking promises of conquest and excess. The pulsing beat of the bass was more than mere sound; it was a heartbeat, a pulse that sped with each whispered bargain, each exchanged a look of unspoken craving. The air was heavy with secrets, dense with whiskey, sweat, and the faint whispers of smoke wafting from the secret corners where power was traded like coins.

This was a kingdom in which the desperate fought for a taste of something more, the strong fed on the weak, and morality was nought but a lost relic. Power here was not born but taken—one cruel stroke at a time. Those who came hoping to find a simple refuge soon found themselves trapped, their desires warped into obsessions, their ambitions honed into weapons.

Mickey had been here previously, a mere witness, attracted by curiosity and the fascination of something out of reach.

Tonight, however, he was not just a bystander. The whispers caught up with him, wrapping around his mind, nourishing the quiet hunger that had always simmered beneath the surface. He had lived on the outside all his life, observing the rich move through the world with an untroubled power, and now, suddenly, for the first time, he could taste it—the tug of something darker, something thrilling. A hand on his shoulder, a sly grin from a face half-concealed in smoke, a glass set before him with an unstated invitation—this was how it started. The world about him receded the rhythm of the club combining with the thudding in his breast. The craving for power, a smouldering ember in the past, now blazed with an inescapable fury. He had crossed the threshold, and there was no going back.

Mickey positioned himself beside the VIP area, eyes scouring the floor strategically. He wasn't present to party or drink. He was here to make deals, to stake his own claim to a world in which survival consisted of more than mere existence—more than breathing, it took power.

Mickey had learned all that from being with Luther: dominance wasn't earned, it was seized, often through violence.

Little Joe, whose name was only whispered in dark alleys and back rooms of the city's underworld, relaxed in the velvety softness of the VIP booth's leather seats. He was not as showy as Luther was but equally so in a subtler sense of his kind of menace. He sat there, waiting for Mickey, the dark amber fluid in his glass slowly circulating in a swirling pattern.

"Mickey," Joe greeted, his voice smooth, his expression unreadable. "I hear you've been making moves."

Mickey smirked, sliding into the seat across from him. "I hear you're looking for an opportunity."

Joe chuckled, taking a slow sip of his drink. "That depends on what you're offering."

Mickey leaned in, his voice dropping. "I want Luther gone. I know you do. We both know his empire is too big, too reliant on men who'd rather be feared than respected."

Joe raised an eyebrow, pretending to be interested. "And you think you can do better?"

"I don't think," Mickey replied, his confidence unshaken. "I know."

Joe studied him for a long moment, his gaze sharp. "Luther isn't just going to roll over. He's survived men smarter than you."

Mickey's smirk widened. "That's because they tried to take him down from the outside. I'm already in."

Joe gave a low whistle, placing his glass on the table. "Bold. Suicidal, but bold."

Mickey leaned back, exuding an air of calculated nonchalance. "You want in or not?"

Joe breathed in and out his nose, slowly, deliberately. "You've got balls, I'll give you that." He hesitated, and then nodded. "I'm listening."

Meanwhile, back in their apartment, Kiera sat frozen, gazing at the untouched wine in front of her. The room was colder and different. Mickey had changed, and she didn't know if she knew the man he was evolving into.

The drive that had propelled him to leave their situation behind was now taking over. It was no longer survival but power and control, and control came at a price.

She had witnessed the change in his eyes, how he stood and talked—less like the man she had fallen in love with and more like the men he used to abhor.

Her phone vibrated. She checked the screen. Kenny.

She hesitated in answering.

"Hello?"

"Kiera." His voice was strained. "You must speak to Mickey. He is making a play on Luther."

She sat bolt upright, her stomach churning. "What? Why on earth would he—"

"Because he believes he can conquer." Kenny expelled a sigh of frustration, exasperation edging his voice. "He is not sane, Kiera. Luther is not someone you betray and live to tell about it."

Kiera swallowed hard. She had tried to reason with Mickey before and show him the dangers of playing this game. But he wouldn't listen.

"I'll talk to him," she said, her voice steadier than she felt.

Kenny hesitated before responding. "Do it fast? Because if Luther finds out first, Mickey's a dead man."

Mickey returned home late that night, the high of the meeting still pulsing through his veins. He had set things in motion. There was no turning back now.

The moment he stepped inside, he knew something was wrong. Kiera stood in the middle of the room, arms crossed and her expression unreadable.

"We need to talk."

Mickey sighed, running a hand through his hair. "Not now, Kiera. I'm exhausted."

"Yes, now." Her tone was hard, unbreakable. "I know what you're doing."

Mickey's gaze flashed with something indiscernible, but he remained silent.

"You're after Luther," she went on. "And it's going to kill you."

He laughed. "You don't get it—"

"No, Mickey," she interrupted. "You don't get it. You think this is about power, about control. But it isn't. It's about staying alive. And you're losing yours."

Mickey gritted his jaw, frustration crossing his face. "I'm not going to waste my life giving orders, Kiera. I'm not going to be just another piece on someone else's board."

She stepped closer to him, her voice gentler now, close to begging. "And what about us? What will become of us if you follow through on this?"

Mickey hesitated. For the first time that evening, uncertainty flashed on his face, only for a moment.

"I have to do this," he finally said, his voice filled with conviction.

Kiera looked at him for a long time, studying his face for any hint of the man she used to know.

Finally, she nodded, her heart falling. "Then I can't watch you ruin yourself."

Mickey's breath was caught. "What are you saying?"

She grabbed her coat, her movements slow but deliberate. "I'm leaving."

Mickey's stomach twisted, but he didn't stop her. He didn't know how.

The door closed behind her, and Mickey felt truly alone for the first time in his life.

Mickey stood frozen in place; his hands clenched into tight fists at his sides as Kiera stormed toward the door. His breath hung up in his throat as he looked at her, the darkness of the room throwing long shadows across the emptiness between them. His life had been one of struggle—one against the world, one against those who counted him out, one against demons that taunted him in the night when city streets were dark and silent. Now, he was losing the one thing that had made the entire struggle worthwhile.

He had always been struggling. As a child, it was fists and pilfered food, bruises on his ribs from nights when his father returned home too drunk to care where the punches landed. Then, it rose the ranks, ensuring no one could ever put him in the ground again. He had worked years earning his right to be here, fighting his way up through blood and treachery to where he stood. And yet, nothing seemed to be of any use. Not if Kiera wasn't here.

Why does it have to end like this every time? The question came uninvited, raw and bitter. Why do they all leave?

His mother had departed—exited the front door on some frigid winter evening and didn't glance over her shoulder once. His other friends had either turned on him or passed on before their time. No one ever lingered. Kiera had been that sole exception. She had been that one reality in his world that had stood firm, concrete. A beacon in the dark when the weight of it all seemed too great to carry.

Now, he could see it in her eyes—the disillusionment, the disappointment. She wasn't merely leaving the room. She was leaving him.

The pain of the sting was intolerable, but he refused to let her see it. He had never begged, never pleaded for anything in his entire life, and he wasn't going to start now. However, as the door closed behind her, something deep within him snapped, a hurt long hidden ripped open again.

Mickey let out a harsh breath, turning away from the door as if doing so would obliterate the sight of her disappearing form from his mind. He grasped the closest glass of whiskey, gulping it down in one motion, embracing the burn that travelled through his chest. That was simpler to pretend it didn't hurt—that he wasn't just that same abandoned child, standing in that empty space, wondering why he never was enough.

He slammed his palms onto the desk, panting, and the crush of his ambition closing in around him.

He had believed power would set all things right. If he owned the city and possessed the money, the terror, the regard, then perhaps he wouldn't have to hurt as much as the worthless child everyone had discarded.

But standing there and seeing Kiera go felt like losing himself again.

And the worst part?

He was aware this time that he could blame no one but himself.

Chapter 9: Luther's Challenge

As Luther entered the poorly lit warehouse, the air reeked of sweat and motor oil. Either side did not claim this territory—at least not yet. Hard-eyed and hungry for blood, a ring of men stood by as Big Joe cracked his knuckles, his massive body throwing a long shadow under the suspended lights.

Big Joe was not simply a fighter but a force of nature. A giant of a man with arms as big as steel beams, his presence was enough to make lesser men stumble. His skin was scarred from innumerable battles, each one a testament to dominance, to establishing that he was the monarch of this subterranean world. His hard and cracked knuckles had destroyed bones and crushed dreams; tonight, they were directed at Luther.

The air around him seemed to vibrate with unspoken menace, a weight that pressed down on those who dared to challenge him. His deep-set eyes, dark as coal, held no warmth, only the quiet, deadly confidence of a man who had never needed to doubt his strength. His sheer bulk made him seem immovable, a human wall of muscle and brute force.

As he cracked his knuckles, the noise was gunfire in the quiet warehouse, a dark threat of the agony to follow. His lips twisted into a sneer—not one of humour, but of confidence. He wasn't here to fight but to remind everyone why he dominated this territory.

"Show us what you have, kid," he growled, his words rumbling deep in the cramped room like a faraway clap of thunder. The circle of men shifted awkwardly, showing their regard for Big Joe by holding their collective breath and expecting the blowout to come.

Luther uncoiled, rolling his shoulders. Now was the time. To become the leader, he had to establish it in this place.

Big Joe sneered, his teeth shining like an animal spotting wounded game. "You sure, kid?

You don't exactly look like you can hold your own."

Luther didn't blink. "I don't have to. Just gotta be better than you."

A stir ran through the crowd, half-humorous, half-eager. The fight was underway.

Big Joe entered quickly, swinging a big hook to knock Luther out. However, Luther had been on the streets for years, learning to move quicker before the pain hit. He ducked, spun, and fired a sharp jab into Joe's ribs.

Joe growled but didn't let up. He swung again, hitting Luther on the shoulder, sending him stumbling. The crowd erupted, the smell of violence hanging heavy in the air.

However, Luther wasn't finished.

He came back fast, employing his smaller size to his benefit, keeping just out of range while raining down sharp, deliberate blows. His fists landed on ribs, jaw, and kidney—each blow eroding the larger man's stamina.

Joe, enraged, lunged wildly. That was enough for Luther. He dodged and struck Joe in the stomach with a hard knee. The larger man stumbled, and Luther took advantage, delivering a brutal uppercut that sent Joe crashing.

There was silence in the warehouse for an instant. Then, the cheers burst out.

Luther wiped the sweat from his forehead and surveyed the room. The men—they belonged to him now.

Across town, in a darkened apartment, Mickey sat over a messy desk, his fingers tapping on the wood. His eyes were on a city map, with Luther's expanding power noted.

"He's getting too big, too quickly," Mickey grumbled, his jaw clenching.

To his side, his second-in-command, Tony, crossed his arms. "So what's the play?"

Mickey smiled a slow, sinister grin. "We locate his vulnerability. In addition, when we do?

We eliminate him before he even knows it's coming."

The game is only just beginning.

Mickey had sat by himself the previous night, a half-full glass of whiskey on the table next to him, his thoughts consumed by Kiera. Her loss nagged at him, a stinging, persistent ache he could not seem to rid himself of. She had been his anchor, the only one who had ever made him feel something more than ambition and power. However, she was gone. And he had no one to blame but himself.

He had attempted to persuade her to remain, vowing everything to her, but Kiera had not been fooled. "I don't want a life founded on blood, Mickey," she said, her voice firm in the face of the pain in her eyes. "I can't stand by and watch you destroy yourself."

And she had walked away.

Mickey interred the pain deep within him as he sat in his office with his men around him. Regret had no place in his world. If Kiera would not stand with him, he would make his empire single-handedly. And that empire would begin with defeating Luther before he was an actual threat.

In the meantime, Luther was partying in the warehouse but was aware that the battle was far from won. Eliminating Big Joe was just the start. He had to cement his grip, acquire more followers, and keep an eye on his back.

While drinking in the bar's backroom that evening, a face he hadn't seen in years appeared in the doorway. A friend from his past, Malik, entered the room, his face impassive.

"You've made a name for yourself, Luther," Malik said, sitting across from him. "But power such as this—it makes you a target. You know that, don't you?"

Luther smirked. "I didn't get this far by being careless."

Malik leaned forward, lowering his voice. "Mickey's planning something. Word on the street is, he's coming for you."

Luther's smirk faded. He had expected as much, but hearing it confirmed it sent a chill down his spine. Mickey wasn't the type to wait and watch—he was the type to strike hard and fast.

Luther took a slow breath. "Then I suppose it's time I begin making plans, too."

The fight for domination was only just starting.

CHAPTER 10:
DESCENT WITH MADNESS

Following Big Joe's vicious murder at Luther's hands, the underworld is filled with rumour. Some think Little Joe is too afraid to strike back, others that he's simply waiting. Either way, Little Joe has been quiet—too quiet.

Little Joe was Big Joe's son and right-hand man, the ex-boss of the North-side drug trade. While his father was a brutal and respected boss, Little Joe never managed to emerge from the shadow of his father. He had the name and the connections but not the raw violence and strategic mind that made Big Joe feared.

Mickey, ambitious now to the point of madness, begins pressuring Kenny for answers. He realizes that if Luther can take out Big Joe, nobody is safe, least of all him. He requires an escape route, an upward path.

The dim, smoky interior of the bar clung to Mickey and Kenny as they huddled in a cramped booth. The evening's drinks had loosened tongues, but Kenny's was still tight with nervous agitation. He leaned forward, his voice a hushed whisper.

Kenny revealed that Little Joe, far from being resigned to grief, was consumed by rage. He wanted Luther's life, but lacked the resources and support to achieve it. He was, in a word, vulnerable.

Mickey smirked, the amber liquid in his glass swirling as he considered the information. "So, he's desperate?" he asked, the word hanging in the air.

Kenny affirmed with a nod. "Desperate men do stupid things. But smart men? They use desperate men."

Mickey reclined, his gaze fixed on the shadows beyond the booth. The possibility of exploiting Little Joe's desperation was already forming in his mind. If Little Joe desired Luther's death, he could be manipulated into an alliance, with only a gentle nudge required. "Arrange a meeting," Mickey instructed, his voice low and decisive. "Discreet. Neutral location. Let's see how desperate he is."

Kenny hesitated, his brow furrowed with concern. "You sure, mate? You screw this up; you don't just have Luther on your back. You got a whole war coming down on you."

A confident smile spread across Mickey's face, his mind already racing through the potential outcomes. "Then I'd better damn well make sure I win," he replied, the words laced with a quiet, dangerous certainty.

The London night air was heavy with tension. Mickey O'Brien perched in the corner of a dingy bar, the low light glinting off his whiskey glass. In front of him, Little Joe, holding his drink, leaned in, his face inscrutable. The two men weren't buddies. Hell, they hardly trusted one another. But this evening, trust was irrelevant—power was.

Luther had become too powerful too quickly. With Big Joe murdered by his own hands, the scales were tipped. Luther ruled the streets, his name spoken in terror. But Mickey noticed the cracks in his empire—the arrogance, the increasing paranoia, the enemies piling up in the wings.

Little Joe wasn't the type to make deals easily. But Mickey saw what everyone else did: Little Joe wasn't his father. He wasn't built for war. Not alone.

"Luther killed your old man," Mickey said, swirling the amber liquid in his glass. "And you're telling me you're just going to let that slide?"

Little Joe's jaw tightened. "You think I don't want him dead? I do. But my father always said—revenge without strategy is just suicide."

Mickey grinned. "Smart man. So let's strategize."

Little Joe let out a breath, drumming his fingers on the table. "What's your angle, Mickey? You've been working for him. What's stopping you from being another one of his puppets?

Mickey leaned forward. "I work for no man. No more." His words were low and menacing. "I don't merely want Luther killed—I want to steal all from him. His business. His contacts. His crown."

Little Joe shrugged dryly. "You're going to march in there and steal it?"

Mickey's smile crept slowly out. "I don't march. I hit."

A long silence stretched between them. Outside, the sound of sirens faded into the distance. The weight of what they were about to do settled over them like a loaded gun.

"How do we do it?" Little Joe finally asked.

Mickey leaned back, satisfied. "First, we break his operation from the inside. You still got men in the North who answer to you?"

Little Joe smiled. "Not as many, no. But the ones I do? They'd kill for me."

"Good," Mickey said. "Because they may have to."

The scheme was straightforward—on the surface. Mickey would stay within Luther's orbit, furnishing Little Joe with information, chipping away at Luther's control before the knockout punch. At the same time, Little Joe's gang would hit Luther's pipelines, shutting down his cash flow.

It wouldn't be swift. It wouldn't be neat. But it would be over with Luther in the ground.

Mickey toasted. "To new beginnings."

Little Joe paused and then raised his own. "To endings," he amended.

They clinked glasses, sealing the bargain.

And in that instant, the war for the throne had commenced.

Later that evening, Mickey sat in his dimly lit office, a hand holding a bottle of whiskey and the other cradling a cigarette. The office was in shambles—papers scattered across the desk, a lamp broken in pieces on the floor, and the stench of sweat and desperation hung heavy in the air. His paranoia had been increasing over the past few weeks, and now it had reached the point where he couldn't shake it.

Shadows crept at the borders of his vision, whispers slipped across the stillness, and every creak of the boards made his heart pound.

His reflection in the mirror was a stranger. The thin man standing before him had wild, haunted eyes, far removed from the smug upstart he remembered. Power, once a desirable fantasy, was now a strangling reality. Money, that once-iconic symbol of success, was now stained with the blood of his enemies. And the blood itself, always a reminder of the savagery he'd embraced, had insinuated itself deep into his core, warping him into a stranger he didn't know.

He barely remembered the climb, the pitiless deals and the backstabbing that brought him to the top. It was a blur of adrenaline and need, an addiction that consumed all in its path. Now, at the precipice of complete control, he was balancing on the edge of madness. The city, which had previously been his to command, was now a labyrinth of paranoia, each shadow concealing a possible enemy, each whispering a threat.

The weight of his crown choked the solitude irreparable. He'd miss the period when his conscience wasn't a battlefield, when his midnight dreams weren't crowded with the faces of those whose lives he'd destroyed. But there could be no going back. The man in the mirror, hollow-eyed and trembling, was all there was left to him. Power had not liberated him; power had ensnared him in a gilded cage he'd built.

A knock on the door jolted him from his circular thoughts. He leaned over to get his gun, pointing it toward the door.

"Who's there?" His voice was raw, throat dry from too much drinking and insufficient sleep.

"It's me." Kiera sounded even, but he didn't believe her. He didn't think anything anymore.

Mickey hesitated before he pushed open the door. Kiera entered, observing the state of the room. She set down a bag on the table, her movements slow and guarded.

"You look like crap," she said, sitting down across from him.

"Thanks." He ran his fingers through his dishevelled hair. "What do you want?"

"I'm worried about you, Mickey."

He snorted sceptically. "No, you're not." He took a deep drag on his cigarette. "You're here because you think I'm going crazy. Because you want to know if I'm still strong enough to hold this together."

"You're right," she said. "But I also want to help you."

Mickey studied her, trying to see the underlying meaning of what she was saying. There was something different about her this evening, something calculating.

"You don't think I see, don't you?" He sneered. "The way everyone gawks at me. They're thinking I'm losing my mind." He slammed his chair out of the way. "They think they can take what's mine."

"No one's taking anything from you, Mickey," Kiera replied quietly. "Unless you allow them to."

His head snapped to hers, and the room whirled. Was it the alcohol? Or was it something else? The shadows shifted and morphed, forming shapes—figures staring at him from the edges. He pinched his eyes shut, but the whispers still grew.

"I need to go," Kiera said, rising. "Just... try to rest, okay?"

Mickey's anger had been building for weeks, but now it exploded into something more sinister—a poisonous mix of desperation and anger. All the friends he had relied on had either betrayed him, deserted him, or been worthless. Kenny had walked away; Paul was AWOL, and Kiera. Kiera had been the hardest blow of all. It wasn't merely that she'd left him—it was how she'd done it, how she'd turned the knife as his world was coming apart.

CHAPTER 11:
THE COUP AND THE FALL

Mickey hated Luther because he perceived him as the last barrier between him and complete control of his absence. From the start, Mickey had been nothing more than a small-time foot soldier in Luther's drug empire—merely another expendable piece. However, he had greater aspirations.

He hated being ignored, aware that, in Luther's estimation, regardless of how much he earned or how big of a risk-taker he was, he would always be nothing but a street vendor. The anger brewed into hatred as he saw Luther dominating with violence, decimating anyone who crossed his authority.

His rule was founded on terror, and his punishments were brutal. Mickey had witnessed men being put to death for small offences, their bodies battered and left like garbage. He knew that as long as Luther ruled, he would never be free—he would always be living in fear of sudden and brutal death.

When Luther began doubting the profits and saw discrepancies in the earnings, Mickey knew the noose was tightening around his throat. Luther had suspicions about him, and the moment that was done, there was only one way it could go. Mickey would either be taken out, or he had to kill first. But it was not just fear and ambition driving his hatred—it was manipulation, too. His girlfriend, Kiera, had fuelled his paranoia for months, getting him to feel he was worth more, that he was the one who was supposed to be the boss.

He wasn't motivated by power alone—he was motivated by the desire to prove himself, to demonstrate to everyone that he was more than a mere foot soldier. But in his zeal to kill Luther, he did not notice the larger game unfolding. He was never the mastermind—merely another pawn being set into place. And by the time he knew it, it was too late.

He would not let it end this way. His eyes were blurred, his heart racing, but his instincts propelled him on, and he found himself in front of the only person remaining who still mattered: Luther, the cause of his despair, the one who had discarded him like refuse.

The air inside Luther's nightclub, usually thick with the revelry of vice, now pulsed with different tension. Sweat, smoke, and the metallic tang of fear hung heavy, a suffocating shroud. Mickey and Kenny sat huddled in a corner booth, whiskey glasses untouched, their hushed conversation a desperate attempt to stay hidden beneath the thundering bass.

Kenny's betrayal wasn't born of loyalty to Mickey but from the raw, gnawing fear that had been his constant companion for years. He'd served Luther not out of devotion but out of survival; each day, a tightrope walked above a chasm of brutal consequences. When Luther's suspicions turned towards him, when the whispers of missing profits and questioned loyalties reached his ears, Kenny knew his fate was sealed. He was a dead man walking. Sensing Kenny's desperation, his fear a palpable aura, Mickey manipulated him with practised ease. He fed Kenny's doubts, painting Luther's reign as a crumbling edifice, promising him a slice of the power, a chance to rise above his role as a mere intermediary.

But Kenny was never meant to be a king, only a pawn in Mickey's ruthless game. He'd chosen his side, not out of belief in Mickey, but because it was the only path he saw to survival. Ironically, it was a choice that would ultimately lead to his demise.

Luther was alone in his office, a solitary figure in the heart of his crumbling empire. Luke was gone, and his loyalty was rewarded with death. His most trusted soldiers were either securing their own corners of the territory or too lost in the haze of their own addictions to care. This was the moment, the window of opportunity Mickey had been waiting for.

Mickey glanced at Kenny, his eyes gleaming with predatory intensity. "Are you ready for this?" he asked, his voice a low, dangerous whisper.

Kenny exhaled sharply, the sound a mix of fear and grim determination. "No," he admitted, his voice trembling slightly. "But we do it anyway."

Mickey smirked, a cruel twist of his lips. "That's the spirit," he said, his voice laced with a dark satisfaction.

Their hands drifted to their weapons, the cold steel a stark contrast to the heat of their fear, as they rose and moved towards the office.

Kenny knocked his knuckles, rapping against the heavy wooden door. A pause, thick with anticipation, followed. Then Luther's deep and lazy voice echoed from within. "Come in."

Kenny opened the door, stepping inside first, a sacrificial lamb leading the way. Mickey followed, closing the door behind them, sealing their fate.

Luther sat at his desk, rolling a cigar between his fingers, his eyes fixed on some unseen point. He didn't even look up as they entered. "You boys look like you got something on your mind," he said, his voice laced with amusement. "Speak."

Kenny's hand twitched towards his gun, his fear overriding his caution. But Luther saw it, his senses honed by years of ruthless survival.

The whiskey glass in his hand flew across the room, a deadly projectile shattering against Kenny's temple. The force sent Kenny stumbling back, a crimson river of blood running down his face, blurring his vision.

Mickey lunged, his knife flashing under the dim light, a desperate attempt to seize the moment.

Luther moved with surprising speed for a man his size, catching Mickey's wrist before the blade could connect. His fist crashed into Mickey's ribs, a brutal blow that sent him reeling, stealing his breath. "You ungrateful little fucks," Luther growled, his voice a low, menacing rumble, as he reached for the gun tucked under his desk.

Still dazed and disoriented, Kenny fired first, a desperate act of self-preservation. The bullet hit Luther in the shoulder, spinning him sideways, his gun clattering to the floor.

Mickey didn't hesitate. He snatched his knife from the floor, his eyes filled with a cold, ruthless determination, and drove it into Luther's ribs. Luther let out a choked gasp, his eyes wide with disbelief and pain. Another stab, and another, each one a brutal punctuation mark on his reign. Blood spilt over the desk, pooling beneath Luther as his breath rattled, a death rattle that echoed through the silent office.

Mickey stepped back, panting, his body trembling with adrenaline. Luther's body slumped against the desk, a lifeless husk. Silence descended, heavy and suffocating.

Kenny held his side, groaning, his face contorted in pain. "You think he's dead?" he asked, his voice a hoarse whisper.

Mickey wiped the blood from his face, his eyes cold and devoid of emotion. "If he's not," he muttered, his voice laced with a chilling finality, pulling the trigger one last time. The shot echoed through the office, a brutal confirmation of Luther's demise.

The club fell silent as Mickey emerged from the backroom, his clothes stained with blood, his face a mask of grim determination. People stared, wide-eyed, as the realization set in. Luther was gone. And in his place stood a new king.

Mickey walked to the balcony overlooking the main floor, his gaze sweeping over the sea of faces below. "I've assembled you all today to discuss the future," he announced, his voice cold and sharp, cutting through the silence. "Me. I am the future."

Murmurs rippled through the crowd. Someone in the back scoffed, their voice laced with disbelief. "What you mean? It don't work that way, you're a nobody—"

Mickey shot him in the head, the sound a brutal punctuation mark on his declaration. The club fell into dead silence, the air thick with fear.

Mickey lowered his gun, his eyes scanning the crowd. "Anybody else want to call me a nobody?" he asked, his voice a low, menacing growl. No one spoke.

Mickey smirked, a cruel twist of his lips. "Didn't think so," he said, returning to the office, the throne now his.

Hours later, Mickey returned to his flat, his triumph tainted by a chilling emptiness. Kiera was waiting, her expression unreadable.

Mickey sighed, pouring himself a whiskey, his movements heavy with exhaustion. "You heard?" he asked.

Kiera nodded. "Yeah. I heard."

Mickey leaned against the counter, grinning, a flicker of his old self returning. "I did it. We don't have to worry about Luther anymore. We run everything now."

Kiera didn't smile. "You run everything now," she corrected, her voice flat.

Mickey's smirk faded, replaced by a look of confusion and anger. "What's that supposed to mean?"

Kiera set her glass down and stood, stepping closer, her eyes filled with a cold, unforgiving light. "You think this is a win, Mickey? You think you're free?" She laughed a hollow, bitter sound. "You're just another Luther now," she whispered, her voice laced with contempt. "And I don't love you anymore."

Mickey froze, his triumph turning to ash in his mouth.

Kiera grabbed her coat, her movements sharp and decisive. "I hope it was worth it," she said, her voice laced with a chilling finality.

She walked past him towards the door, her footsteps echoing through the silent flat.

Mickey clenched his jaw, his voice a desperate plea. "Kiera—"

She didn't look back. The door clicked shut.

And for the first time, being king felt like nothing at all.

Somewhere in the city, Kiera sat in a darkened restaurant, stirring her wine as she gazed at Luther's smirking face. Part of him was utterly proud of how he outsmarted Mickey. On the other hand, Kiera had spent months fuelling Mickey's paranoia, whispering into his ears, sowing tiny seeds of madness. She had seen him fall apart, piece by piece until his mind was as broken as his hold on reality.

"It's working," she said quietly. "He's coming apart."

Luther leaned back in his chair, his fingers tapping rhythmically against his glass. "Good. Keep prodding him. When he's weakest, we'll take it all."

Kiera allowed herself a slow, knowing smile. Mickey had never been hard to manipulate. He had always trusted too easily, felt too deeply, and reacted impulsively. Now, he was drowning in his own mind.

Before he knew the truth, it would already be too late

But the question is: how did Luther survive?

CHAPTER: 12
THE MADNESS FOR POWER

The night of the attack...

Two henchmen put Luther's slumped body in the back of an unmarked van. Inside, there was the stench of blood and gasoline and the muted growl of the engine covered up their low-pitched whispers.

"Boss is finished," one grumbled, readjusting his hold on the body. "No way is he ever going to wake up from that."

The other laughed. "Good riddance. Now Mickey's the boss."

A low, coarse gasp punctured the night.

Then another.

The enforcers did not have a chance to even react before Luther's eyes sprang open. His hands reached out, locking one man's throat in their grip and jerking him backwards, the gory crunch of bone echoing through the van. The second guard reached for his gun, but Luther was quicker, pulling him forward and battering his head against the metal wall.

The van skidded wildly before coming to a screaming stop. The driver had hardly a moment to react to the mayhem before the rear doors exploded open. Luther stumbled out into the night, covered in blood and gasping for air.

He'd made it through.

And he wasn't finished yet.

Luther had always predicted betrayal, his fists as sharp and calculating as his mind. When Mickey and Kenny attacked him, he was severely injured but not killed, his survival an affirmation of his resilience and resourcefulness. His body was spirited away by his most trusted alliances, who simulated his burial so that the world could believe he was dead, a ghost roaming in Mickey's conscience.

For weeks, he had lain low, healing in a safe warehouse on the city's outskirts as Mickey filled his position, his conceit and brashness serving him well. Luther knew Mickey was too arrogant, reckless, and inadequate to cling to power long. All he needed to do was wait, to allow Mickey's paranoia to get the better of him, to allow his ambition to tear him down from within.

With Kiera's assistance, he would shatter Mickey's mind before shattering his body, a vicious and deliberate revenge that would reduce him to a shell of his former self.

The club, which had been a discord of Luther's rule, now reverberated with a nervous quiet. Mickey's rule had started, but the triumph tasted hollow, a ghost limb of the power he desired. The men, their faces clouded with an agitated unease, glided like spectres, their allegiance as fragile as glass. The money poured, a river of ill-gotten wealth, but the respect, the visceral, raw fear Luther inspired, was missing, substituted by a wary, calculating acquiescence.

Mickey slumped in his office, the lavish room now a gilded cage, a pile of money and cocaine littering the desk like a grim still life. He filled a glass of whiskey to the brim, his shaking hands pouring it until it sloshed over the edge of the rim. The burden of power, which had been so far away from him as a dream, now weighed him down with oppressive might, more massive than he ever could have envisioned. Kenny was gone a victim of his own ambition. The faces that reflected his ambition now reflected a glacial fear, a thin currency that might turn against him at any second.

The first time Mickey saw Luther's face in the mirror, a ghostly vision out of the corner of his eye, he attributed it to a trick of light, a ghost born of fatigue. However, the second time, the vision was bleak and irrefutable. Luther sat in the chair opposite him, his formerly imposing form now a ghastly apparition, blood still oozing from the wound in his throat, a mocking sneer curling his lips. "You really think this is your city?" he breathed his voice a cold echo in the silence.

Mickey, his nerves strung out, his mind bordering on the brink of sanity, threw the glass at the chair in a last-ditch effort to destroy the illusion. But the glass exploded against the wall, not leaving so much as a smudge of dampness and the eerie feeling of dread. Nothing was there, no tangible shape of his enemy, only the haunting sound of his voice and the cold memory of his uncompleted business.

Sleep was a luxury he could no longer indulge in, a dangerous terrain where nightmares blended with reality. Food tasted like ash in his mouth, and the flavour of guilt and fear was an ever-present, bitter aftertaste. The walls of his empire, once a testament to his victory, now seemed to shut in on him, the silence making his paranoia whisper louder. In the stifling silence, he heard Luther's laughter, a derisive, otherworldly sound ringing through the desolate halls of his mind.

Kiera observed Mickey's gradual decline into madness in the background, her eyes flashing with a chilling detachment. He didn't even realize that she remained in communication with Luther and didn't have a clue that the delusions were not simply the product of his broken mind but stage-managed deceptions constructed to shatter him.

Late in the evening, when Mickey would give in to fatigue, his body weak and defenceless, Kiera would give him heavy injections of LSD, stoking his paranoia, distorting his perceptions, and pushing his mind further into the depths. His already fragile mind, battered by the constant stress, the corrosive impact of drug use, and the nagging sense of guilt for what he was doing, started to shatter totally, the cracks opening wider with each day. Each shadow in his office appeared to shift, contorting into monstrous forms, muttering threats in Luther's tone. Each voice in the club, once a symphony of greed and ambition, now echoed Luther's, a chorus of censure.

Mickey spent one evening alone in his office, staring at his reflection in the dark screen of his TV, which was off, looking for a glimmer of the man he used to be. Then Luther's voice, hard and threatening, sounded behind him. "I allowed you to live in my world, and you thought you could steal it from me?"

Mickey turned round, pistol in hand, his steps jerky, panicked. But there was nobody, nothing but emptiness and a hollowness of sound that stretched his terror further. He panted for breath in wild, convulsive gasps, his frame shivering, his head balancing at the very cusp of non-being. He was going crazy, sliding down the slope, and Kiera and Luther didn't want it any other way.

One night, Kiera sat across from Mickey in their apartment's kitchen. He shook with paranoia, his hands trembling, his eyes blazing with a frantic, haunted gaze. "You're not well, Mickey," she whispered, her voice dripping with a manufactured concern. You need to sleep."

Mickey massaged his eyes, his actions tired, his voice tinged with a desperate urgency. "Each time I close them, I see him. He's not dead, Kiera. I know he's not."

Kiera reached across the table, squeezing his hand softly, her touch comforting. "Then let's ensure it," she whispered, her voice a chilling vow.

She gave him even higher doses that night, more than she ever had before, pushing him deeper into his madness. Under the influence, he began seeing Luther everywhere—in mirrors, shadows, and reflections. The more he saw Luther in the shadows, in mirrors, in the corner of his office, the more he believed that maybe, just maybe, Luther had survived. Every small noise, flickering light, and whisper in the club showed Luther was still watching him. While some of them believed Luther had gone for long, the other said otherwise.

By the time he woke up, it was too late.

Luther was coming for him.

And this time, he wasn't a hallucination.

CHAPTER 13: THE JACKAL'S ARRIVAL

Heavy and ghostly, a low fog spread over the city streets, curling around the amber light of streetlamps like spectral fingers. The flashing neon sign of a late-night takeaway sent jagged, wild shafts of colour onto the rain-soaked pavement, a grotesque kaleidoscope of the mayhem in Mickey's disintegrating mind. A faraway siren moaned, a wailing, otherworldly cry, a dirge for the sanity he was fast losing, dying away into the stifling quiet.

Footsteps reverberated through the fog, slow and deliberate, every step a cold metronome marking off the seconds of Mickey's fading tranquillity. A figure stepped out of the churning mist, his shape twisted by the streetlight's beam. The Jackal. His trench coat, a black shroud to the night, flapped in the bitter blasts of wind, his hat yanked low over his eyes, showing only a glimmer of the feral intensity that burned inside him.

He stood in front of the doorway of a sleazy club, his eyes hard and calculating, taking in the scene with the predatory fascination of a hunter who had already tagged his prey. His lips twisted into a sadistic sneer, a knowing smile that held the promise of pain and revenge. Then, with a cold intent, he moved forward, disappearing into the gloom.

In Mickey's office, the room was an ebony tomb lit only by the erratic, dancing gleam of a single, unshaded bulb. The leather chair groaned beneath Mickey's bulk as he leaned forward, elbows planted heavily on the messy desk, a whiskey glass shaking in his hand. A single bead of sweat ran down his temple, a cold, damp tear against his skin. His other hand, shaking, followed the traces of white powder smeared across his upper lip, a futile attempt to hold on to the temporary oblivion it provided. His brain was a tempest-tossed sea, paranoia gnawing at the fringes of his vision, distorting reality into a grotesque parody of his own terrors. The distant bass of the club throbbed beneath him, a relentless, primal beat, like the heart of some unseen hunter hiding in the darkness.

A knock resonated in the room, hard and demanding, a brutal break into the crushing quiet. Mickey flinched, his muscles coiling, the glass in his hand trembling unsteadily. He cleared his throat, imposing a rough semblance of composure on his voice.

"Who is it?" he growled, his voice abrasive.

A heavy silence hung in the air, charged with an unspoken threat. Then, a cold, deliberate voice cut through the stillness.

"Officer Jones. CID."

The words cut through the air like a knife, a shivering announcement of doom to come. Mickey gulped hard, his heart thudding like a caged beast. His fingers clutched the glass, his knuckles whitening, as he managed a grimace that didn't reach his eyes.

"CID? What's this about?" he queried, his voice tinged with a manufactured swagger.

The door groaned open, and there stood the Jackal in the doorway, his form outlined against the faint light of the hall. He stepped into the room, moving with an unnerving, unhurried pace, his extremely shiny shoes making hardly a sound on the wooden floor. His dark, emotionless eyes locked onto Mickey's, an unblinking emptiness of cold malevolence.

"We must talk about Luther," he whispered, his drawl low and menacing.

There was a flicker of terror, a slight crack in Mickey's well-placed facade, revealing his fear. Mickey froze, but the Jackal's gaze was too sharp; he had registered the subtle shift. He never missed a thing." I don't know what you're saying," Mickey faltered, desperation in his tone.

"Oh, but you do," the Jackal whispered back, his voice low and menacing. "His body was found, wasn't it?"

A pregnant silence filled the space, broken only by the violent thudding of Mickey's heart.

"Bodies don't stay buried forever," the Jackal said, his voice dripping with a cold certainty.

A single bead of sweat ran down Mickey's neck, a cold, damp path across his skin. He leaned back in his chair, pretending to be relaxed, but his knuckles were white around the glass, giving away his inner struggle.

"Unless you've got a warrant, you can fuck off," he snapped, his tone filled with a forced swagger.

The Jackal's smile widened, slow and deliberate, a chilling expression that never reached his eyes. "Oh, I'll be back," he said, his voice a low, menacing promise.

He turned on his heel, his steps smooth and fluid, and left the room, his steps almost silent as he melted into the darkness. He did not glance back. He did not need to. He knew he had already sown the seeds of fear in Mickey's mind.

Mickey staggered into his apartment, breathing in harsh gasps, his eyes wide, mirroring his turmoil. The apartment was a pandemonium, a testimony to his deteriorating sanity. Bottles were strewn on the floor, and white powder was etched on the glass coffee table in lines that resembled chalk on a tombstone. His hands shook as he rubbed them through his hair, talking to himself in a mumbling tone that was hardly understandable and a last attempt at grasping the fragments of his sanity.

Then, a whisper, a hushed, ominous voice, came from across the room, a cold whisper from the back of his mind.

"You think you can bury me?"

Mickey's breath caught in his throat, his heart pounding inside his ribs like a bird behind bars. He looked around frantically for the source of the voice, but there was nothing, just shadows, trembling and black, laughing at him.

"Go screw yourself..." he said, his hoarse, shaking voice barely above a whisper.

He reached for a bottle and swallowed the scalding liquor in a reckless attempt to stifle the horror that consumed him. He smacked his shaking hand against his lips, eyes tightly shut, panting. When he finally opened them, Luther stood looming behind him, his image reflected back from the mirror, a phantom shadow of his guilt.

Mickey shrieked an animal scream of fear and hurled the bottle at the mirror. glass exploded, splinters raining like stars falling, mirroring his shattered image, fragmented and ugly.

He staggered out of the apartment, his breath fogging in the night air. His coat was hanging off one shoulder, his shirt open halfway, and his gait unsteady. He was mumbling to himself, his fists tightening and loosening, and a desperate struggle to maintain the shreds of his broken reality.

His eyes, previously aglow with ambition and guile, now reflect an empty, haunted look. He is a man unravelling, a spectre of his past, lost at sea in paranoia and terror.

Out of sight but always observing, the Jackal stood witness in the darkness, his smirk lingering, unspoken evidence of his reign over terror.

Kiera's phone jolted its piercing ring, cutting through the stillness of her apartment. She hesitated, her gaze locked onto the instrument, before answering.

"I need help," Mickey begged, his tone a wheedling whisper.

Kiera's jaw hardened, her tone icy. "You're past help, Mickey."

"Please... I don't know what's real anymore," he pleaded, desperation etched in his voice.

Her fingers clenched on the phone, her face hard and unrecognizable reflected back at her from the black window. "You deserve everything that's coming," she said, her voice cold and merciless, and hung up.

Behind in his office, the silence was a stifling pall, dense with the horrors of Mickey's fear. Slumped in his chair, he crouched the unbuttered bottle of whiskey a bitter reminder of the oblivion he could not attain. Knotted in his hair, his fingers pulled in anguished frustration, a silent scream at the agony that devoured him. He barely knew the man he had become, a haunted spectre tortured by the ghosts of his own past.

Then, the knock, a solid, insistent rap that broke the tenuous silence, sent a shiver of raw terror through him. His breath stopped, his body bracing, every muscle wound tight like a spring ready to break. He stared at the door, his heart thudding against his chest, a wild drumbeat against the silence.

"You ready to talk now?" the Jackal's voice boomed, low and menacing, a chill threat of vengeance. Mickey's throat tightened, a parched, painful spasm. He couldn't speak, couldn't move, and couldn't even breathe. He was trapped, a cornered beast, paralyzed with fear. The room narrowed, the walls closing in upon him, the air becoming heavy and smothering. A prisoner in his office, a victim of his own greed, and the Jackal, the hunter, waited at the door to take his rightful payment.

CHAPTER 14:
THE RECKONING

The dim bulb projected long, waltzing shadows over the debris of Mickey's flat. Beer bottles were scattered like fallen marines, their contents gone from the air hours before, with only a clinging residue left. A fine white powder, the spectre of his spiralling addiction, dusted the glass top of the coffee table, a stark admission of his tenuous control.

Mickey leaned back in a worn armchair, his face in his hands, and the burden of paranoia weighing him down like a tangible load. The city, once his to command, now seemed a crushing cage, its walls shutting in with each tick of the clock. He massaged his temples, attempting to suppress the throbbing pain that thudded behind his eyes, but the ghostly whispers in his head became louder and more urgent, fuelling his mounting fear.

A metallic click sliced through the fog of his self-imposed exile. The door groaned open, and Kiera stood in the doorway, her figure backlit by the faint hallway light. She was holding a syringe, the needle glinting menacingly in the dark. Her face was hard, expressionless, without the warmth he remembered, now replaced by an icy detachment that made his spine tingle.

"What's that?" Mickey rasped, his eyes flickering with suspicion. He shifted in his chair, his body tensing, watching her every move, every subtle shift in her posture.

"Something to help you see things clearer," Kiera replied, her voice flat and emotionless, devoid of any hint of sympathy.

Mickey's eyes narrowed, his distrust deepening. "I don't need your help," he retorted, his voice laced with a defensive edge.

"Oh, but you are," Kiera replied with a subtle bite of nasty satisfaction. "You're losing hold, Mickey. The city is slipping away from you, and you don't even realize it."

Mickey glared at her, his jaw setting, but his hand shook as he wiped the sweat from his forehead. He knew she was correct. The whispers in his head, the perpetual fear, the increasing sense of unreality—it was eating away at him, destroying his sanity.

Kiera advanced, the needle shining in the dim light, a hungry glint in her eyes. "You're attempting to fuck with me," Mickey charged, his tone filled with desperation.

"You already fucked yourself," Kiera sneered, her tone heavy with contempt. "I'm just here to complete the job."

Before Mickey could move, Kiera attacked her actions quick and precise. The needle drove into his arm, a stinging pain followed by a rush of dizziness that swept over him. His breath caught, his eyes widened, and the room started to blur, the walls stretching and curving, the shadows twisting into monstrous forms. He felt himself losing himself, falling into a pit of blackness.

Kiera retreated, regarding him with aloof interest as he descended into madness. His eyes went blind, his perceptions drenched by a maelstrom of wrenched sounds and images. He was losing himself, plummeting into a well of blackness.

A black emptiness lay out before him, an endless stretch of nothing. Whispers slithered through the void, their voices whispering in his brain, weaving a cloth of paranoia and terror.

"You thought you could bury me?" a voice resonated, cold and cruel, Luther's voice.

Mickey spun around, his gaze raking the blackness, but there was nothing. Only the emptiness, a blank canvas of fear. A chill sweat coated his skin, his heart thudding against his ribcage like a caged bird.

Luther stepped out of the shadows, his form half-lit, half-hidden in darkness. His smile was hard, feral, a cold reminder of the man Mickey had betrayed.

"You were never in control," Luther sneered, his voice ringing in the emptiness, a poisoned whisper that stabbed at Mickey's heart.

Mickey recoiled, his head shaking, his mind in turmoil, unwilling to believe what he was witnessing. "You're dead," he stuttered, his voice shaking.

"Am I?" Luther replied, his eyes glinting with wicked mirth.

Mickey's breath trembled, and his body twisted with terror. The walls of the void throbbed, contracting and expanding as if alive, seeking to crush him, to strangle him in his own fear.

Mickey flailed wildly, overturning bottles and sending the glass coffee table crashing to the ground. His body jerked, his limbs thrashing, his mind trapped in the hellish landscape of his own creation.

Kiera stood over him, arms folded, face impassive. She was a silent witness, a puppeteer manipulating his downfall. She had engineered this fall into madness, feeding his paranoia, playing on his vulnerabilities, all to take the reins for herself.

"Get out of my head!" Mickey wailed, his voice hoarse with horror, a frantic shout swallowed by the vast expanse of his mind.

Laughter resounded in the room, Luther's laughter rebounding from the walls, enveloping him, choking him. It was an irony, an orchestra of his own demise.

Mickey reached for Kiera, his actions slow, and his body against him. He fell, his body twitching, his sight fading, his world shattering, breaking into a million pieces of terror and remorse.

CHAPTER 15:
THE FINAL CONFRONTATION

The bass pounded, a raw, relentless beat that ought to have shaken through Mickey's skeleton but instead was muffled, far away, like the fading beat of a heart struggling, falling into the void. The nightclub, a whirligig of revolving bodies and blinding lights, was a choking cage, its atmosphere heavy with unspoken fear. Once radiant and strong, his universe had narrowed to a stifling room described by paranoia, by the horrifying whispers that resonated in the blackest recesses of his mind: Luther.

Mickey stood at the balcony, alone amidst the celebrations, the city's bright sprawl a harsh mockery of his anguish. His whisky, a clumsy attempt to calm his nerves, shook with agitated violence in his hand, the liquid bubbling against the glass. His eyes swept round the crowd of faces below him, each pair a possible antagonist, each ghost in the heaving shadows. Each flash of light, every unexpected movement, made his nerves jump with the fear that this time it had come; it was inevitable.

He was a predator trapped, a king minus his crown, and his senses cranked to an apocalyptic pitch. The whispers, the ghostly tingling, had evolved into a horror symphony. Then he spotted him.

A man stood still in the evil light of the red lights around the bar. Luther.

Mickey's breath caught, and a strangled gasp stuck in his throat. His heart pounded against his ribcage, a wild drumbeat amidst the quiet of his terror. *It couldn't be.* He held the railing, his knuckles white as the iron dug into his skin. His mind yelled in denial, a wild litany of unknown truths: Luther was dead. He had ensured it. He had driven the knife home into his flesh, felt the resistance, and seen the life ebb out of his eyes. He had witnessed the scarlet stain spread, the last shuddering breath.

Yet, there he was, upright, observing a ghost in the machine—a ghost with a cold smile.

The glass slipped from his shaking fingers, shattering on the gleaming floor, the sound a harsh, jarring note in the humming music. Luther lived. The unthinkable had occurred, the dead had risen, and Mickey's meticulously built world was falling into dust.

A wave of sickness swept over him, a cold sweat bursting on his flesh. He shoved through the throng; his movements were jerky, and his breathing laboured. He was a puppet whose strings had been cut, his body acting of its own will, spurred by a raw fear. Once a background to his dominance, the music seemed warped, otherworldly, a cacophony of fear. Faces blurred, lights spun, and the world tipped on its axis, becoming a dreamlike, hellish terrain.

He arrived at the bar, his gaze desperately scanning for the ghostly presence, but Luther was nowhere to be seen. *No. No, no, no.* The denial chanted into his mind, a desperate battle against the closing in of the madness. He spun about wildly, his eyes scanning the room, but the faces were nothing more than faces, hollow and unaware, swept up in the hedonistic vortex of the night.

Then, a chillingly familiar voice cut through the noise, a whisper that felt like a blade against his skin.

"You look like you've seen a ghost."

Mickey spun around, his heart leaping into his throat, and there he was—Luther, alive and whole, his dark eyes burning with malevolent amusement. The sight sent a raw terror through Mickey's body, a visceral, animalistic fear that paralyzed him.

He stumbled backwards, his voice a rasping whisper. "You—"

Luther leaned his head to the side, his grin spreading, a menacing smile chilling Mickey. "Me?"

Mickey's vision blurred, the edges of his sight darkening. His body felt heavy and sluggish, the effects of Kiera's poison, the slow, insidious drip of drugs that had eroded his strength, his will, his very being. He was a broken man, a shadow of his former self, trapped in his nightmare.

"You're dead," he whispered, his voice barely audible above the music.

Luther smiled a slow, sadistic smile and showed Mickey the full extent of his meanness. "Am I?"

Mickey flung himself at him, a wild, awkward try to hit, to show that he wasn't cracked, that there was still some strength left in him. But Luther evaded with ease, gripping his wrist in a vice-like hold.

With a bitter twist, he slammed Mickey into the bar, the impact shaking his bones, the breath forced from his lungs. Luther held him pinned against the unforgiving surface, his gaze burning into Mickey's, cold, unblinking.

"You actually thought you could kill me?" Luther's voice was quiet, controlled, a predator playing with its quarry. "You thought you could steal my throne?"

Mickey fought, his brain a shattered mess, his thoughts churning in a haze of terror and drugs. He was trapped, powerless, at the mercy of the man he had attempted to murder.

"I—" he started, but the words stuck in his throat.

A vicious, sharp knee to his stomach sent him stumbling, doubling over in agony. The crowd, in their own world of alcohol and music, hardly saw the fight, their eyes glassy, their actions mechanical.

Luther seized Mickey by the collar, his hold like iron, and started pulling him through the club, a ghastly procession through the crowd of blind dancers. Mickey stumbled, his legs unsteady, his mind spinning, struggling to keep pace as Luther pushed him through the crowd.

They came to the balcony, the city's lights spreading out beneath them, a great, uninterested sea of neon and darkness. Luther pushed Mickey back against the iron railing, the chill metal cutting into his flesh.

"You never deserved any of this," Luther spat, his words dripping with venom. "You were a king in your own mind, but you were just another rat."

Mickey struggled against Luther's hold, his mind yelling at him to fight, to do something, but his body refused to obey. He was a machine broken, his gears stripped, his circuits burned.

He was too weak. Too broken.

Luther brought his face close, his breath hot against Mickey's ear, his voice a cold whisper, the last thing he would ever hear.

"Tell Kenny hello for me."

And with that, Luther pushed him off the ledge.

The wind whooshed past Mickey's ears, a scream of endings and a howling symphony. The lights ran together into smears of colour, a kaleidoscope of dizzying whorls of his ending world. For the first time in the long, dark journey through the nightmare, he felt weightless, released from the crushing burden of fear and suspicion.

Then darkness took him, an endless, gaping void, and the last curtain dropped on his sad, broken tale.

Chapter 16:
The True Victor

The music had ceased. The people had disappeared, leaving only a heavy silence against the walls like a clenched breath. The air reeked with the acrid smell of blood, lingering like cheap perfume, choking in its tenacity. Neon lights stuttered overhead, their greenish glow cascading over the dance floor where Mickey has shattered form was stretched out in a grotesque pose of finality.

Luther stood at the balcony, his chest expanding and contracting in great heaving breaths, the adrenaline still coursing through his system. His knuckles were white where they clung to the rusted railing as he looked down at the man who had struggled for years to steal everything from him. Mickey was a used pawn in a game he had never really comprehended.

He had clawed his way to the top, ruthless and unrelenting, only to tumble like the others.

Luther breathed hard, wiping the sweat from his forehead. The burden of victory weighed on him—a crushing, inevitable thing. He had won. He had reclaimed what was his. The city was his once more.

Or, so he believed.

A crisp, metallic snap reverberated through the empty quiet behind him. A noise he recognized all too well.

Luther did not shift initially. He did not have to. A gradual smile creased his lips as he relaxed his posture, easing the tension from his shoulders before he turned around.

"You never really learn, do you?"

The voice was smooth, even. Lacking hesitation.

Luther returned her stare, his smirk growing slightly wider. The gun in her hand did not flinch. Her dark eyes, ever watchful, were inscrutable in the darkness.

"Kiera," he panted, still trying to breathe.

"Come to thank me?" He asked, smiling up at her.

She advanced, slow and measured. Her face remained the same, but something in her presence had a weight more substantial than the gun in her hand. "I came to finish this."

Luther chuckled, shaking his head. "You think you're any different than us?"

Kiera's grip tightened, the gun's metal reflecting the pulsing neon. "No," she admitted, her voice almost too quiet, too calm. "But I'm smart enough to walk away."

Luther's smirk faltered. A flicker of something—understanding? Fear?—crossed his face.

"You think this ends with me?" he said, voice lower now. "You kill me, another man steps in. That's how this world works. You don't win, Kiera. You just postpone the inevitable."

Kiera's fingers tightened on the trigger. "No. I end the cycle."

Her mind returned to the nights spent seeing Mickey come apart at the seams due to Luther's influence. How he had become the man, she loved and was transformed into a beast who beat her, broke her, and took everything from her—including their unborn child. The streets, the power, the greed—it all traced back to Luther, the puppeteer tugging on strings, turning men into beasts.

She pulled the trigger.

The gunshot cracked the silence, a sudden and vicious explosion that echoed through the deserted nightclub. The impact of the bullet threw Luther backwards, his body lurching as though struck by lightning. A sudden, stifled breath caught in his throat as he slipped his hand flying to his chest where the bullet had ripped through clothing, skin, and bone.

His fingers came away wet with blood.

He attempted to say something, but the words just would not surface. His throat constricted, eyesight blurring as the pressure in his chest became heavier, choking. His knees buckled under him, and the universe turned sharply sideways as he collapsed.

The blow was vicious. A gut-wrenching thud rang out across the empty space as he came down inches from Mickey's lifeless body. Two men who had battled tooth and nail for dominance were now nothing more than corpses on a crimson floor.

Silence.

Kiera slowly released a breath, lowering the gun. Her hands shook, but not out of fear. Out of release. Out of the burden of a choice made at last.

For the first time in years, she was free.

Kiera had understood that Luther was the mastermind of the brutality that ruined her life, corrupting Mickey and transforming him into an abusive monster who eventually led her to lose their unborn baby. She understood that men such as Luther would perpetuate as long as no one was there to stop them, and murdering him wasn't merely a matter of vengeance—it was ensuring no other Mickey was born.

She had witnessed how Luther's hold on the city turned men into monsters, compelling them to serve or be destroyed by him. She wanted to get out but realized that she would never be free as long as Luther was alive. Unlike the ones who fought for dominance, Kiera did not want to dominate; she tried to flee, and Luther's death was the only means of ending the cycle and taking back her life.

She unhesitatingly walked over Luther's body, her boots making red impressions on the ground. The door to the office was before her, a doorway to the remnants of his empire. In it, piles of money and narcotics were strewn about the desk, the war spoils in wait to be taken.

She grabbed a duffle bag, shoving it with money and anything else she could fit. Not because she wanted it—but because she was owed it. Because after all those years of playing at someone else's game, she was finally taking something for herself.

The fire exit waited at the back of the room. The city lay beyond it, alive with possibility.

She could vanish. Begin anew. Be something—someone—else.

She slung the bag across her shoulder and walked through the door, cool night air embracing her.

She did not look back.

The city belonged to nobody now.

And for the first time, she wasn't running away from it—she was walking away from it.

EPILOGUE

The city had always belonged to men like Luther—until it didn't.

The streets were quiet now, though not because of peace. It was a quiet born of the aftermath of spilt blood, of the last resonations of a once-magnificent empire spent in the biting chill of the night. The underworld had realigned itself, and the ones who had commanded it had died, every one of them.

Kiera didn't wait to see the aftermath. She had made up her mind long before the night she fled.

She stood before the window of the small flat she had taken for the duration, her suitcases full and waiting. She had no time to dally. The city, its wounds, and its darkness had nothing to offer her. She had done her part, seen men kill themselves over-ambition, and now she was finished.

Luther was dead. She made sure of it.

It wasn't vengeance. Not quite. It was survival. Ensuring she was not another statistic in the long, vicious game that had taken so many lives before her. She had watched Mickey slide, watched ambition drown him. And she had learned, finally, that men like Luther didn't disappear—they needed to be wiped out.

No one witnessed her departure. That had been her plan. No sweeping goodbyes, no goodbye kiss-offs. Only the soft scuff of her footsteps over the broken sidewalk as she vanished into the darkness was just one of the many spectres this city had produced. She carried cash, a passport, and a destination. She wouldn't look back. She couldn't.

But what she left behind was destruction.

Luther's throne sat empty, a kingdom without a king. And power, like nature, hated a vacuum.

Mickey thought he was ready. He thought he could slide into Luther's spot and dominate the streets just like his mentor. However, Mickey never really appreciated the burden of the crown he so frantically wanted to don. He clawed his way to the top only to discover that it was a lonelier, more perilous place than he had envisioned. His adversaries orbited like vultures, men who were once his friends now tallying how rapidly they could carve a slice of his empire for themselves.

Luke was gone and disappeared into the night. Kenny had been discovered in a river two weeks earlier, another victim of the game. And Mason, the veteran of the city's underworld, had read the writing on the wall. He knew what was on the way.

You won't survive," he'd said to Mickey when he departed. "Not because you're not intelligent, not because you're not as hard as I am. But because you believe you can play this game and win. Mickey had scoffed then. Now, standing in the club that once belonged to Luther, staring at the empty seat where the man used to hold court, he felt it. The weight. The paranoia. The certainty that his time was running out before it had even really begun.

Men met below the city in a secret, smoky room. They were the real power players, not just people following orders.

"What now?" The question hung in the air, thick with unspoken ambition. A cruel smile twisted a man's lips. "Now? We see who dares to claim the prize."

They knew the truth. London belonged to the ruthless, the cunning. Luther and Mickey, kings in their twisted realms, had fallen. The city, hungry for a new master, waited.

"You think she's gone for good?" A question, sharp as a blade, sliced through the silence. Kiera. They had underestimated her. A mistake they wouldn't repeat.

The radio crackled a faint echo in the car's quiet interior. Kiera's mind raced, a whirlwind of possibilities.

Would she disappear?

Change her name?

Find a quiet corner of the world and vanish?

Or...

Her gaze flickered to the duffle bag—the cash, the product, the power. London had taken everything, but it had also offered a gift, a chance, a choice.

A slow, predatory smile spread across her face. Her foot pressed down on the gas. The car surged forward, devouring the miles, and Kiera, for the first time, felt the thrill of true, untamed freedom. The game was far from over.

Key Takeaways

From this guide, the following conclusions can be derived:

- The quest for power can be all encompassing and ultimately corrupting. Mickey's insatiable ambition takes him down a dark road, having him turn against his loved ones and sacrifice his values. He gets so addicted to his need to control that he forgets what is of value in life, eventually losing dearly for it.
- Power corrupts, and absolute power corrupts absolutely. The higher Mickey rises in ranks, the more ruthless and tyrannical he becomes. He misses his power, treats the people around him poorly, and eventually becomes the same kind of person he loathed. This reflects the corrupting effect of power and the need to remain humble and moral even when in leadership positions.
- Our decisions affect us and other people. The actions of Mickey have a snowball effect, affecting not only his life but also the lives of the people around him. His betrayal of Kiera, for example, results in her disillusionment and heartbreak. Likewise, his brutal quest for power instils fear and insecurity in his organization.
- Real strength is not in dominance but in empathy and compassion. Compared to Mickey and Luther, Kiera is a character who personifies real strength. She is aware of the uselessness of violence and the need to end the cycle of retaliation. She prefers a path of peace and self-restraint, proving that real strength is not in brute force but in empathy and compassion.
- The value of being true to oneself and one's principles. Kiera is the moral compass throughout the story, reminding us of being true to our values even in the face of tough decisions. Her choice to leave Mickey and set out on her own path indicates her value to her own good and her unwillingness to compromise her values.

- The cycle of violence and the need to break it. The guide shows a world in which violence leads to more violence, and in which seeking power results in bloodshed and devastation. Kiera's decision to leave such a world behind implies the need to break this cycle and forge a different one, one that values peace and compassion.